UP, UP AND AWAY SUSIE

Susie and her mother and father are going to visit Susie's grandparents. For such a long trip, Susie will need to have her very own suitcases, packed with lots of things to take with her.

"Don't forget Teddy," says Susie's mom. It's his first plane trip, too!

Finally, Susie and her family are ready. In the car and off they go!

At the airport, Susie sees people rushing every which way. Some have just landed and are looking for taxis and buses. Some are leaving, and looking for the ticket counters.

Then the family goes through security. Susie walks through the metal gate while a special camera looks right through her handbag. Teddy has to go through the gate too!

"Let's go to the gate where our plane will take off from," says mom. They walk quickly through the terminal, past the shops and restaurants and other gates.

Susie and her parents find their gate. "Flight 447 now boarding!" they hear. They've made it on time!

Susie hands her ticket to an attendant.
"Have a nice flight!" the attendant says.

"Be sure to keep your seatbelt fastened," says
Patty. "Plane rides can get very bumpy."
Susie tightens her seatbelt around her waist.
Teddy wears one, too.

Patty explains the buttons above Susie's seat. "One is a light switch, the other blows cool air, and the third is to press if you need me."

At last they're ready to take off! Susie feels the plane moving faster and faster, and then, whoooosh! The plane is in the air!

Susie looks out of her window. Everything on the ground is getting smaller and smaller as the plane goes higher and higher into the sky. Fluffy white clouds are everywhere.

Patty comes up the aisle. "Time for lunch!" she says, taking a tray from the cart she's wheeling. She shows Susie how to pull down the table from the seat in front of her and put her lunch on top of it.

"Prepare for landing," comes the pilot's voice from the cockpit after everyone finishes lunch. Susie looks out of the window. Everything on the ground is getting bigger again. She can see houses and streets and trees below.

After the plane lands, Patty comes back up the aisle. She
pins something on Susie's dress.
"For being one of our best passengers, we're awarding you
your own wings," Patty says. "You should feel very proud!"

At the arrival area, Susie and her parents pick up their lugage. Susie watches all the different suitcases ride along the carousel.
"Here come ours!" she shouts.

They find Susie's grandparents waiting with big hugs and kisses. "How did you like your first ride in the sky, Susie?" they ask.

"It was the best ride I ever had," says Susie, "especially because it brought me here to you!"